(Them Boys: Book 1)

Alexandria House

Pink Cashmere Publishing, LLC
Arkansas, USA

Pink Cashmere Publishing, LLC
pinkcashmerepub@gmail.com

Set - a god of chaos, fire, deserts, trickery, storms, envy, disorder, violence, and foreigners in ancient Egyptian religion

1

Kareema

When I see you, you better not be wearing panties.

I tucked my lips between my teeth to keep from laughing out loud at his text, and then replied with: *Or what?*

Him: *Or I'm gonna rip them or poke a hole in them. Your choice.*

Me: *Poke a hole with what?*

Him: *My dick!*

Me: *Um, the last time I checked, it wasn't sharp enough to poke a hole in anything.*

Him: *It ain't about sharpness. It's about hardness. Like right now? I'm thinking about your pussy and my shit is hard enough to bust concrete.*

I actually did laugh at that.

Me: *I got work to do. I'll see your silly ass tomorrow.*

Him: *Can't wait.*

Me: *Me either.*

As I placed my phone on my desk, the door to my office flew open, and the only somebody who could get away with busting in there stepped inside. Seeing the look on her face, I sighed. "Since you're allergic to knocking, could you at least close the door before you say whatever you're about to say?"

With a huff, she eased the door shut. I watched as her shoulders lifted and fell, her back to me.

Somehow, I managed not to roll my eyes as I asked, "What is it, Tori?"

Finally turning to face me again, she crossed her arms over her chest. "Yolanda needs to go. She's...she's being divisive."

"Yolanda is my best teacher. I'm not firing her because she has a child by your new man."

"That's not why she needs to be fired. She has a bad attitude!"

"With who besides you?"

"So you're not going to fire her?" Her eyes were wide with genuine shock.

"No."

"But—Mama! I can't work with her!"

"You have your class, and she has hers. You *don't* work with her."

She stared at me and I stared right back.

"But—" she tried again.

"Tori, when I hired you, I told you there would be no special treatment. I'm not firing a great teacher because you have personal beef with her over a negro who isn't good enough for either one of you. And why exactly does he have your car today?"

That made her leave, as I knew it would. She

failed to close the damn door, though, so I was left vulnerable to any complaining parents who might happen to pass my office while on their way to pick up their precious babies, and since my only child had exhausted what little patience I had left this late in the day, *I* closed it. A week didn't go by where she didn't make me regret giving her a job, but that was more for me than her. She'd dropped out of college and now had a three-year-old son to take care of, so either it was give her a job or keep dealing with her sitting around my house doing nothing.

But she was so damn spoiled—my fault. And entitled—also my fault. And lazy—her father's fault.

With his sorry ass.

I was a hustler, always had been. I merely kicked that into overdrive when I finally got rid of his ass.

His *super* sorry ass.

Sighing again, I told myself not to think about him and to concentrate on wrapping up the business of the day instead. I had to fight not to say fuck it and leave, because all I wanted to do was get on a plane and make my way to my escape. Yeah, that's what he was, the man with the concrete-busting dick, I mean—*he* was my escape. Shit, in more ways than not, he was my salvation. He saved me from destruction every time I saw him, every time I was in his presence, and that was more than a little frightening. In my experience, a man with that much power, that tight of a hold on your heart, was a dangerous man.

Downright deadly.

Shaking off those thoughts, I made myself wrap up my paperwork, and once I was sure it was late enough for the building to be empty excluding me, I began gathering my things, hoping my favorite nail tech hadn't left my regular salon yet, because I was in desperate need of a mani and a pedi. Unfortunately, I'd miscalculated the time of my escape, because no sooner than I'd stood from my desk and swung my purse over my shoulder did a knock sound at my door, a timid knock. Dropping my shoulders and my head, I sang, "Come in," unenthusiastically.

It was Tori, wearing a sheepish expression as she opened the door and slid into my office with my grandbaby on her hip. I loved that baby despite the fact that at forty-one, I was too damn young to be a grandmother.

"Hey, baby cakes," I cooed, reaching for my grandson. "How's Gigi's baby?"

"Good," he said, planting a sloppy kiss on my cheek.

"Aw, thanks for the sugar, punkin'!" I said, turning my attention to Tori. "What can I do for you, Tori?" If she was looking for a babysitter, that was out. I loved Lil' Man, but I needed to prepare for my trip.

"Nothing, I mean…" she sighed. "I'm sorry about earlier."

"Apology accepted," I stated, trying to hide my shock.

She smiled, relief on her face as she said, "Monté said I'd feel better if I apologized and he was right!" After that declaration, she reached for the baby, and after planting him on her hip again, added, "Have fun on your trip, Mama." Then she left, and all I could do was shake my head at it taking her man to talk some sense into her, a man who barely had any sense himself.

Shit, where did I go wrong?

I was only nineteen when I had her. Maybe that was it.

Before I slid all the way down the rabbit hole of regret, I left, making it to the salon just in time to get my nails done.

******

I hated airports and flying. I really did, but since this little arrangement with my guy started, I'd found a tiny bit of joy in the rituals of checking luggage, going through TSA, waiting at gates, and praying I didn't end up seated on the plane next to a jerk or someone with poor personal hygiene. And if I scored a window seat? Well, that made for the *best* flight.

As I sat in the gatehouse a full hour before boarding began, I smiled about what had become the best part of my life, my mini baecations with my part-time man. Not part-time as in he had a wife or a girlfriend other than me—at least I didn't think he had one—but part-time as in when we were together, it was literally everything. *He* was everything. But we lived separate lives, and that was the way we both wanted it.

I stopped daydreaming, pulled out my earbuds, and was in the middle of watching a YouTube video on my phone when a call popped up on the screen—my BFF Tricia.

With a smile, I answered her call. "Yes, I made it on time, and I'm sitting at my gate."

"So you're calling me predictable?" she squawked.

"When it comes to checking up on your oldest and dearest friend, you are, and I love you for it."

"But you don't love me enough to tell me who your vacation bae is after three damn years. You acting like you're messing with one of them bad-ass Mitchell boys."

I chuckled. "What made you think of them?"

"I don't know. Because they were such damn terrorists back in the day, always fighting and getting into trouble, I guess. Damn demons. I suppose you keeping this nigga a secret like his ass is wanted by the FBI all this time made me think of their probably-in-jail asses."

With a smirk, I asked, "How do you know he's black?"

"Because I know you, hooker! Been knowing you longer than everyone, including your baby daddy."

"You tryna make me vomit? Why'd you have to bring his ass up?"

"My bad. Anyway, I know your sometimes bae is a negro because every time you come home from one of these fuckations you always have that big black dick glow."

"Trish?"

"Yeah?"

"I'll talk to you later."

"Okay, tell Shu Mitchell I said hey."

Shaking my head, I ended the call and navigated back to the YouTube app in search of a good fashion haul.

*****

I ended up with a got-damn middle seat and spent the flight shrugging Mr. Window Seat's uncontrollable sleepy head off my shoulder and trying not to notice the aisle seat guy's incessant sniffing. I hoped I didn't catch anything from his ass.

I gotta stop buying these cheap-ass plane tickets.

I was so relieved when the plane landed that I was among the folks I usually criticized for hopping up the second the "fasten seatbelt" sign was turned off, damn near climbing over the aisle dude to make my escape, and felt like twerking when I was finally able to step off the plane and into the terminal.

At my arrival gate with my carry-ons slung over my shoulder, my eyes rounded my immediate surroundings. Surprisingly, this airport was one of the quieter ones I'd ever been in at that moment, quiet and not nearly as crowded as I expected it to be. I should've been able to easily spot him, but I didn't see him anywhere. We'd said we were meeting at my arrival gate, hadn't we? Had he gotten the wrong information from the monitors? Or was he running late? Had something happened to him? An accident?

I was already nervous, because I was in *his* town and would be seeing *his* home for the first time. Now my ass was panicking on top of the anxiousness. Biting my bottom lip, I stepped from the gatehouse onto the walkway. Still no him. Through a heavy sigh, I pulled my phone out of my bra — yes, my damn bra — to see if he'd texted me while I was in the air and almost jumped out of my skin when I felt an arm slip around my waist but smiled when my braids were moved and lips met the side of my neck as the scent of his cologne enveloped me.

"Where were you?" I asked, as he held me in the middle of the walkway, forcing people to navigate around us.

"In the restroom. Had to take a piss," he said in that panty-dropping, gruff voice of his. Then he spun me around, gripped a handful of my ass, and proceeded to explore every centimeter of my mouth with his tongue. When we parted, I was dizzy, my eyes glued to him as he licked his lips, took possession of my hand, and said, "Come on."

2

Set

I smacked Kareema's ass cheek, clutched a plug of it, and growled, "Whose pussy is this? Huh?" It was an unfair question, but she knew to answer it.

"Oh, got damn! It's yours!" Her voice vibrated from the impact of me plowing into her with long, deep strokes.

"Say my name, Kareema!"

"Set!"

"This pussy belongs to who?"

"Set!"

"You got-damn right!"

I closed my eyes and kept stroking, trying not to bust, because being inside of this woman felt so damn good that I lost a little more of my sanity and my will to do anything other than fuck her every time we were together, which wasn't often enough. And we were never together long enough when we were together, either. But this was what it was, and wasn't shit I could do to change it.

"Set! Shit!" she moaned, her face in the pillow

as she threw her ass back at me. I felt the orgasm when it hit her, felt her walls squeezing my dick, felt the liquid she squirted splash against me and roll down my thighs, felt my damn nuts tingle, and before I could get ahold of myself, pull out, stop stroking, do anything to delay the end of what we were doing, I fucking exploded, and that felt almost as good as being inside her.

Blowing out a breath, I fell onto my back, closed my eyes, and threw my arm over my forehead. "Shit!" I mumbled. Then I opened an eye, grabbed Kareema's limp body, and pulled her on top of me.

*****

It wasn't until I woke up that I realized the pussy had knocked me out. I instantly missed her weight on my body and sat up, my eyes racing around my bedroom. I could tell through the closed blinds that the sun was setting, and shit, she was probably hungry and in my kitchen looking for food. At least I hoped she was and that she hadn't left. She'd been real hesitant to come to my city and stay at my place. Maybe she'd left, gone to a hotel?

Climbing out of bed, I hit the toilet before

pulling on my boxers and leaving my bedroom, quickly finding her in the living room. I smiled a little and blew out the breath I'd been holding as I stepped behind her and placed my chin on her shoulder. "What you doing?" I asked.

"Just checking things out," she replied, reaching back to touch my head as I kissed her neck.

I wrapped my arms around her. "Yeah? You like what you see?"

"Mm-hmm. I wish I could've seen one of your matches."

I lifted my eyes to the display case she was staring at full of pictures of me in my prime along with a pair of my boxing gloves and my belts. "For real? You wish you'd seen me get fucked up?"

Turning to face me, she raised her eyes to meet mine. "Um, from what I heard, you were doing the fucking up."

I grinned. "Yeah, but it wasn't always pretty for me. Besides, I wasn't the same back then. You got the best version of me."

"Do I?"

I stared at her for a moment before nodding. "Yeah, you hungry, baby?"

"Starving. You screwed all the nutrients out of me. My ass is probably anemic *and* dehydrated at this point."

I laughed and grabbed both her ass cheeks. Kareema didn't have a huge ass. It was proportional to her slim body, but it was so soft that I couldn't keep my hands off of it. Everything about her was perfect, including those titties she swore were too big and didn't match the rest of her body.

"Well, let me order us some food and replenish your energy, 'cause I'ma need some more pussy," I said.

She smiled. "You want some more already?"

After I'd kissed her, I replied, "Hell, yeah."

Kissing me back, she said, "Tricia brought you and your brothers up today."

"Word? You thank her for...this?"

She giggled. "No, I didn't, but I definitely should have. Her ghosting me that night was truly a good thing."

With a lopsided grin, I said, "Come on, let's order some food."

"Yessir, Mr. Mitchell."

3

Kareema

Three years earlier...

Standing in the doorway of the event center, my stomach lurched. I didn't exactly have fond memories of high school, had skipped the five, ten, and fifteen-year reunions, and was only here, at the twenty-year celebration, at the insistence of my lifelong best friend, Tricia Gurley, whose ass was MIA. She hadn't answered my texts or phone calls, and standing there staring at my classmates doing what they'd always done—clique up—I felt like as much of an outcast as I had all those years ago.

I was the smart, quiet girl who blended into the background, camouflaged by shyness and cloaked in low self-esteem. All of those feelings came rushing back as my eyes perused the crowded room bathed in green and white and full of tables, a buffet line, a dance floor, and a godawful cover band playing Alanis Morrisette's *You Oughta Know*. Deciding that I could either keep standing there like a moron, leave, or find a seat, I opted to step deeper into the room and locate a chair to sit in and rest my feet since I'd gone all out to look like someone other than the old Kareema Sperry, donning a black wrap dress and heels that were way out of my comfort zone in height. Fortunately, I found a table with just one guy sitting at it, one *fine* guy. I could recognize that even in the dim lighting.

"Uh, is this seat taken?" I yelled over the music, pointing to one of the five empty chairs at the table.

He stared at me for a few seconds before shaking his head no.

"You mind if I sit here?"

Again, he shook his head, and in response, I plopped down in the chair and released a sigh of relief as the feeling returned to my feet.

"I'm Kareema Sperry, by the way," I said to the handsome man I didn't recognize, but then again, there were nearly five hundred people in my Caruso High School graduating class.

"I know," he stated in a gruff voice that inexplicably made my pussy water like an onion-fumed eye.

"Oh, you do?" I asked, genuinely surprised. Shit, I didn't think anyone knew me besides the teachers and Tricia.

He nodded. "Yeah, we had Coach Benton's World History class together."

"Oh, wow! You must've really changed. I

don't recognize you. What's your name?"

His eyes left my face and focused on something beyond me, then refocused on me. "Set Mitchell."

Ohhhhh, shit.

No wonder so many seats were available at his table.

"Oh…" was all I managed to say. Now I could see it, the toasty brown skin and those eyes that fueled rumors of the Mitchell boys being part Asian. Set's were the same brown as his skin, which had always seemed weird to me. Now? Those damn eyes made my belly jump.

He gave me a grin that didn't quite reach his eyes. "You can leave if you need to."

I actually thought about it, because even though twenty years had passed since I'd last seen him, the Mitchell name still struck fear in me. With the mention of that name came the gossip, stories about the three brothers triple-teaming anyone who looked at them the wrong way. The brothers were mean, loved to fight, and terrorized the female population of the school, or so I'd heard. I was never foolish enough to get any firsthand knowledge, though. Nevertheless, my damn feet were still angry at me, so I said, "My throbbing feet say otherwise. Besides, you look harmless enough." That was a damn lie. He looked fine, *sexy*, and the way his eyes were drilling holes into mine was anything but harmless.

A melodic chuckle escaped his mouth. "I ain't exactly harmless, but I ain't everything y'all think I am either."

Kicking my shoes off under the table, I lifted my eyebrows. "Who is y'all?"

"The whole damn class. A gang of people done sat at this table and damn near ran away when I told them who I was. Winston Coleman almost tripped over his own feet tryna get away from here."

Since Winston had always been an arrogant asshole who thought he knew it all, a notion bolstered by his position as class valedictorian, I laughed. "I woulda paid money to see that."

"It woulda been worth it."

I smiled. "So...what have you been doing all these years, Set Mitchell? How are your brothers? You married? Where do you live? Kids?"

"Got damn, is this a job interview or something?"

I shrugged. "Just curious to know what one of the most feared people I've ever known has going on."

"I ain't realize you knew me."

Why did that make my pussy do a triple Salchow? Had to be that damn voice of his. He had one of those rough-ass DMX voices. "Okay, *knew of*. I wasn't messing with you back then. You scared me, to be honest."

"Yeah, well…I guess I was a little fucked up back then, but I ain't never hit no girls. That shit was a lie. My daddy woulda beat my ass. He didn't play that."

The Mitchell patriarch was a cop, a big intimidating man who wasn't to be messed with just like his three stair-step sons—Set, Jah, and Shu. If I remembered correctly, Set was the oldest, followed by Shu, and then Jah.

"That's good to know," I replied.

"Yeah. So I'm not married, never been married, got one son who is eighteen, I'm a retired professional boxer, and I own a gym now, work as a personal trainer. I live in Vegas. My brothers are good. Shu was in the military, but now he's got a good factory job. Jah's a mechanic. They both still live here."

"A boxer?"

He shrugged. "I always liked to fight, but you know that, huh?"

I shrugged.

"So what about you, Kareema Sperry?"

"Married twice, single now, one daughter, a newborn grandson, I own a daycare, and I live here…still. I don't have any siblings."

He nodded. "You look good, gooder than a motherfucker, actually."

My pussy did a double, no, a *triple* Lutz this time. "Thanks, so do you."

After staring at me for a moment, he asked, "Wanna head out with me, go get a drink? This got damn music is making my head hurt. Hell, the least they could do is play some Eminem if they wanna keep it Caucasian."

I mean, the constant grunge and emo music *was* a bit unsettling, but I'd just arrived, was supposed to be meeting Tricia who was most likely somewhere dealing with her man and his public domain dick, and this was *Set Mitchell*. In addition to all of that, past instincts shouted at me to say no, but instead, I slid my uncomfortable shoes back on and fixed my eyes on him. "Where to?"

We went to *Ten10*, a bar I'd never stepped foot in that had been a fixture in my city since I was a kid, sat at the bar, and soon, the liquor had helped us transition into an easy conversation. Set was smart, attentive, a grown-ass man that I'd probably still see as a school terrorist had it not been for Tricia ghosting me.

"Two husbands, huh? They *both* fucked up?" he asked, as he peered over the rim of his glass of whiskey at me.

I took a sip of my second rum punch and sighed. "Well, husband number one's name should've been Fuck Up—immature, lazy as fuck, and had the nerve to cheat on me while he was unemployed for the thousandth time. My daughter was like two when we divorced, but you know what? I don't think it's fair to count him as a husband since I married him when I was eighteen."

He chuckled. "Where'd you meet Fuck Up?"

"In high school." I cleared my throat and dropped my eyes. "I married Shawn Thomas."

"Oh, shit! How'd a girl like you end up with him? Y'all ain't even from the same universe!"

Rolling my eyes, I said, "I knooooow. Tricia dragged me to some party at the skating rink, he was there, and I guess he noticed me and my titties for the first time."

"So you like bad boys, huh?" he asked, with one raised eyebrow.

"Puleeze. He grew up in the hood, yeah, but Shawn was all bark and no bite. You should know that. Didn't you kick his ass once?"

"Nah, he wasn't about that life. Talked all that shit in front of folks, and when it was time to get down, the motherfucker didn't show up."

"Oh."

"See, you can't believe everything you hear, Kareema."

"I do see."

"And husband number two?"

"He died five years ago. Cancer. He was a good man, though, treated Tori, my daughter, like she was his own."

"I'm sorry."

Through a sigh, I said, "Me, too."

"You gonna get you a husband number three?"

"Hell no! You ever getting you a wife number one?"

"Fuck no! I like my freedom, love living alone. I can't stand for motherfuckers to be up in my space."

"I know that's right!" I held my glass up as if toasting his sentiment and took a swig of my drink. "I'm used to being alone now. Don't think I could deal with someone in my space either."

"See, you get me." He held his glass up. "Fuck marriage and relationships and all that shit."

Clinking my glass against his, I agreed, "Yeah, fuck alllll that!"

He drained his glass and set it on the bar. "You were so quiet back in the day. Guess you outgrew that shit, huh?"

"Yep, like you outgrew kicking asses."

He smiled and so did I. Then we just sat there looking at each other, our eyes transmitting some shit that didn't make sense but was real. Our attraction and nearly palpable chemistry were very, *very* real.

He was wearing a dress shirt and slacks, but those clothes did nothing to hide the muscles covering his tall body. There was a shadow of facial hair on his face, hair neatly cut into a low fade, thick lips, and those got-damn monochromatic eyes. My God in Zion! Set Mitchell was fucking appetizing.

"Kareema?" he almost growled.

"Yes?" I responded, lifting my eyes from the open collar of his shirt to his face.

"I always thought you were pretty. You're still pretty. Fine, too."

My mouth dropped open. "Well, since I was too scared to look at you back in the day, I'll just say thank you and that you are truly handsome and exceptionally fine right now."

With a huge grin, he said, "Thank you, and I can't get mad at you not wanting to look at me. I earned that reputation. I was a fool, a hot head, and I legit have no idea how I avoided getting arrested other than the respect other officers had for my pops."

"Shit, I thought you *did* get arrested."

Through a laugh, he said, "No, but Jah has an extensive arrest record. Pops couldn't save his ass."

"I can see that. Of the three of you, Jah was the most intimidating and the biggest."

"And he's the youngest." He shook his head.

"Yeah, I thought he was. What about Shu?"

"That nigga's like a ninja. He's big like me and Jah, but you know he's always been quiet."

"Yeah…"

"And he's so quick, he can kick an ass and be gone before the person knows what hit him. Never got caught in his shit."

I laughed and he shrugged with a silly grin on his face.

We both fell silent as we finished our drinks, and when he broke the silence with, "Wanna come to my hotel room with me, Kareema?" with a look of total and complete lust in his eyes, the logical portion of my mind screamed, "No!" However, my vagina, which was in desperate need of maintenance after a five-year drought, was controlling my mouth.

So I said, "Yes, I do."

Set

In my room that night, I kind of lost my nerve. Kareema was and always had been so pretty. I used to stare at her in class but knew she was a good girl. I also knew I had no business messing around with a good girl. I'd been fucking since I was twelve, had a jacked-up childhood, and spent high school trying to fight my way to…something. Peace? Shit, I still don't know. And in that hotel room, half drunk, I wasn't sure if I deserved to be with her any more than I did in high school. Evidently, she sensed the shift in my mood.

"You don't…you changed your mind?" she

asked timidly, pushing my mind further into the past.

"About what?" I questioned.

With a shrug, she said, "Well, I assume you didn't invite me to your room to study the Bible."

I had to smile. "No, not that."

"The Quran?"

"Nope."

"A boy scout manual?"

I laughed. "You wildin' now."

"Well?"

"No, I haven't changed my mind." I was standing there with a noticeably rock-hard dick so I couldn't deny that I wanted her even if I didn't deserve to have her.

Stepping close to me and resting her hands on my chest, she uttered, "Great, because it's been a while for me. I was going to be very disappointed if you'd changed your mind."

I stared down at her, at her round face, thick lips, eyes nearly hidden behind the thick lashes of her lowered eyelids, and I kissed her, my hand on the back of her head, my fingers digging through her hair to her scalp. She moaned, wrapping her arms around my neck and pulling me closer to her. I can't lie; from the moment Kareema appeared at my table, I'd had thoughts of fucking her fine ass, and from the way she was pulling my dress shirt from my slacks and fumbling with the buttons on it as we kissed, it appeared she'd had the same thing on her mind.

"Hold up," I said, backing away from her. "This ain't gotta be a sprint unless you got somewhere else to be. Slow down, baby."

She was breathing hard, her eyes falling from my face to my crotch. "I haven't had sex since my husband died. I don't have to be anywhere else, but I do need you to hurry up and fuck me."

Shit, since she put it that way…

I damn near tore that shirt off of myself, was out of my pants and underwear in a fucking millisecond, and had helped Kareema undress in record time when I stopped and stared at her. Those titties were a got damn work of art. Big and full and —

"You are fucking fine as hell," Kareema muttered as she bit her bottom lip.

"You too, baby," I said. "Kareema, you ain't drunk, are you? I don't want you to do this drunk."

"I'm as sober as a church mother. I ain't no lightweight, Set Mitchell."

"You sure?"

She answered me by grabbing my face and kissing me. So I said *fuck it*, led her to the bed, laid her on it, and strapped up, figuring she didn't have the patience for prolonged foreplay. Stretching my body over hers, I attempted to slide inside her with a mouth full of her right titty, but couldn't.

Five years? Shit, she was as tight as a virgin.

"Relax, Kareema," I whispered, kissing her neck.

"I *am* relaxed. It's—it's always like that. It's a problem, I guess. You have to work your way in."

My dick was so hard now, I was sure I could pound a nail into a wall with it. But instead, I slid down her body and covered her entire pretty pussy with my mouth, licking and slurping on her clit until her legs clamped tight around my head and she released a bunch of unintelligible words. Then…then she *squirted,* she squirted all over my got-damn face, and all I could do was blink and fucking gawk at her pussy in amazement.

"You didn't tell me you were a squirter," I said, licking the fluid from my lips.

"I'm s-sorry. I should've told you," she whined, as she reached down and covered her pussy with her hands, her legs still trembling.

"It's all good," I said. Shit, it was *better* than good.

I moved her hands and settled between her thighs again, making use of the slickness I'd worked to create. As wet as she was both inside and out—hell, she was wet before I ate her pussy—I *still* had to work my dick inside her, but once I got in there?

Motherfucking got damn!

I had never, *ever* felt anything like it, had to close my eyes and concentrate to keep from crying, because it felt so good. I slid in and out of her, her pussy gripping my dick with each stroke, and I felt like I was going to lose my mind. When I felt her walls begin to quiver around me, felt warm fluid shoot from her *again* and hit me as I held her titties together and sucked both nipples at the same time, I jerked and whimpered and filled the condom.

Minutes later, as we lay side by side on the bed, both breathing loudly, she asked, "What the hell are you mixed with? The folks that made the Kama Sutra?"

"Both of my parents are black. My black-ass daddy gave me these eyes along with a lot of other shit."

"I wasn't talking about the eyes. I was talking about the dick. Shit!"

I chuckled, but I'd be damned if I didn't feel the same way about her pussy.

4

Kareema

Now…

I took in the view of terrain that was so different from the green trees and grass I was accustomed to as we ate on his balcony. It was beautiful, beautiful and hot, but what I'd always heard about dry heat being different from the strangling humidity signature of the south was true.

"You like the food?" Set asked, his voice making my stomach quiver. I was too damn old and had been through too much shit for his mere voice to affect me like that, but I couldn't help it. It'd been like this since the first time he touched me three years earlier.

"Yeah, it's really good," I said.

"Not as good as the wings from Tasha's back home though, huh?"

I grinned. "Nah, but they're close. These taste like the building probably passed health inspection. Tasha's probably doesn't even have a damn permit or license or whatever."

He threw his head back and laughed, Adam's

apple bobbing up and down, elbows on the table, hands gripping a half-eaten chicken wing. This forty-one-year-old motherfucker was only wearing his boxers, and his chest looked so good that I wanted to slather wing sauce on him and lick it off. He was just so damn fine!

His eyes were still laughing when he bit into the wing again and stared at me as he chewed.

I took that moment to ask a question that had been occupying my mind since he invited me to visit his home a couple of months earlier. "What am I doing here, Set?"

He stopped chewing and frowned. "Huh?"

"You don't like people in your space, but here I am, all up and through your space. Why?"

He wiped his hands and mouth with a napkin, raked his eyes over me sitting across from him in a bralette and shorts, and finally said, "Because I want you here."

"So you changed your mind about not wanting folks in your space?"

"No. I still don't want folks in my space, but I do want *Kareema* in my space, in my bed, on my face. I love it when you squirt on my face, Kareema. I *love* that shit."

I cleared my throat and took a swig of my soda. "Let's go back to bed, Set."

*****

A week after the twenty-year class reunion that morphed into a weekend of mind-blowing sex with the infamous Set Mitchell, I was sitting in my office at the Kinder Kuties daycare center avoiding paperwork and perusing social media on my phone when my eyes widened. Set and I hadn't exchanged phone numbers. I just left his hotel room and went back to my regular life. He did the same, and I thought it was over, but there I sat staring at a friend request from him that I quickly accepted. As an infestation of butterflies filled my belly and my pussy began doing the Running Man, I toured his page, analyzing picture after picture, and found that as fine as he was now, he was even finer when he was at his boxing prime.

But he was fucking mouthwatering then *and* now.

Shit!

As I followed a link he'd shared to an article about the grand opening of his gym, a private message from him popped up that I read in his voice: *Thanks for accepting my request.*

Me: *Of course. How've you been?*

Set: *Good. You?*

Me: *Good.*

And that was it, our first post-fuckathon conversation. Soon we were messaging each other every day—making small talk, sharing funny memes. Then he invited me to a business trip he was taking to Atlanta one weekend a couple of months after the reunion, and I said yes. I don't know what business he had in Atlanta, though, because we spent nearly every waking moment in bed, naked and screwing. That's when he began to become an addiction for me. Hell, the very thought of him made me sweat and squirm. After that, we exchanged phone numbers, Set invited me on more trips, and what was supposed to be a one-time hookup between two people who were both miles away from wanting a relationship became an…arrangement. When we were together, we were together, but we held no expectations, there were no rules or voiced possession of one another, just monthly or bimonthly baecations, many within driving distance of my city. Okay, so he had a habit of asking me who my pussy belonged to and I had a habit of telling him it was his, but that was just some heat of the moment stuff. Anyway, I had no idea what he did or who he was with when we were apart. I only cared about what I felt when we were together.

Let me stop lying. I was always relieved not to

see him posting other women on social media, which he never did. And as far as the heat of the moment thing? Oh, he literally owned my pussy. I'd mentally signed the title over to him the first time he touched me. No other man had touched me since then, but I knew it was best he didn't know he was my only source of that kind of pleasure. There was no need in putting that on him. I mean, neither of us wanted more than what we had. I know I didn't, despite the fact that I was in love with him. Madly, deeply, desperately in love with him.

5

Set

"How'd you get this scar?" she asked, as her soft finger traced the raised skin that ran from the top of my back to the middle. We were back in my bed, full and exhausted from another round of sex. I was lying on my stomach, facing the window, because I knew if I looked at her, my face or dick was going to end up between her legs again.

"Knife fight," I mumbled. "Tenth grade. The motherfucker said he was gonna cut my spine out of me."

"Damn."

"Yeah, you shoulda seen him when I got through with him. I took that knife from him and fucked him up."

"You-you killed him?!"

"Naw. Lay on my back."

"Why you always want me to lay on you?"

"Why you always asking me that?"

"Because you never answer me."

"Fine. Because you feel good. Come on, now."

I could hear her smile as she said, "Well, turn

over so I can lay on the front of you. Lying on your back always seems strange."

"Ain't nothing strange about feeling your titties on my back."

"Wow, you really love these midgets, don't you?"

"Mm-hmm."

A second later, she was on me and I moaned a little.

"You are so damn strange, Set Mitchell."

"You like it."

"Maybe...hey, are you lying in the wet spot."

"Yep, and I love it. I love how messy your pussy is. Just be squirting all over the place."

"It's gonna soak through to your mattress."

"Good."

"See, weird."

"Mm-hmm."

"Set?"

"Hmm?"

"I-uh...I—"

The ringing of a cell phone interrupted her. Scrambling to get off of me, she evidently grabbed her phone, and said, "Shit, it's just Tricia."

"Answer it," I stated, as I turned on my side to face her.

She shook her head. "She doesn't want anything. Probably just gonna be nosy."

I gave her a lopsided grin. "She still in the dark about us, huh?"

She shrugged. "We're not her business."

"Right."

"Have you…do any of your friends know about us?"

"No."

"See?"

"Yeah."

Silence, and then, with her eyes on her phone, she said, "She's watching my house for me. Maybe I should call her back."

I shrugged. "Go ahead, baby."

She blinked before tapping the screen of her phone and putting it up to her ear. "Trish? What's up? Everything okay there?"

Her eyes darted from me to the wall above my headboard. When her eyes found me again, I smiled and scooted over to her. She was right. From her side of the conversation and Tricia's greeting of "Guess what this nigga just said," that I was able to hear through the phone, she really didn't want shit, so I didn't see a problem with putting Kareema's right titty in my mouth. Damn, I loved those juicy motherfuckers.

She gasped as I sucked her titty like a newborn starving tiger, but she didn't stop me, because she loved shit like this.

Freaky ass.

Squeezing her other breast, I kept sucking as she let out a soft whimper and slid her hand to the back of my head, saying, "Uh, shit…Trish, I gotta—"

Tricia never stopped talking. I could still hear her loud ass through the phone that was pressed to Kareema's ear. So I left her titty wet and glistening from my mouth and kissed her so deeply that she actually dropped the phone. Damn, I loved her mouth.

And Tricia's ass kept talking.

We both forgot about the phone when I eased her onto her back and worked my way into her pussy, her always tight, always wet, squirting-ass pussy.

Yeah, I loved the shit out of her pussy, too.

I loved the shit *and* the hell out of it.

Tricia's faraway voice provided the background noise as I rocked into and out of Kareema, my mouth glued to her neck.

"Oh, shit!" she hissed. "The-the-the phone, Set. I need to—got damn, you feel good!" She was trying to whisper but was damn near shouting.

I sucked her neck, her chin, and her tongue as I glided in and out of her and groped for her phone, finally finding it and taking my mouth from Kareema's long enough to tell Tricia, "Kareema gon' have to call you back." Then I powered her phone off. She lifted up, wrapping her arms around my neck and kissing me as we both moaned. Shit, I think I might have shed a tear or two.

I fucked her long and hard, my ears full of the

sounds of me invading her wetness and my grunts and her whimpers, my nose full of her scent mixed with mine, my eyes rolling to the back of my head as I felt damn near drunk off her pussy.

After we'd both screamed and growled our way through our orgasms, I fell on my back and stared at the ceiling as she climbed on top of me just like I liked for her to. I rubbed her back as I felt her heart race at a pace to match mine.

I loved the shit, damn, *and* hell out of this woman.

I really did.

*****

Two years earlier…

"Set! Set, wake up!"

My eyes popped open in the darkness of the hotel room, my heart fucking hammering in my chest, my breathing loud. I was confused at first, not sure why she woke me up. Then I remembered the dream, wondered if I was acting it out in that bed.

"Kareema?" My voice was so damn high, I barely recognized it myself.

"Yeah…"

"I didn't hurt you, did I? Did I hit you?"

"No! Were you dreaming about hitting me?" she squeaked.

I sat up on the side of the bed and rubbed my forehead. "Naw, never mind. I don't know why I asked that. Shit."

Standing from the bed, I ducked into the bathroom. It'd been a while since I'd had one of those dreams, years, and it shocked the shit out of me that I had one while with Kareema. I never felt anything but good with her, which was probably why I kept making up excuses to see her. This weekend we were in Kansas City, and I was fucking this trip up.

When I finally stepped out of the bathroom, there was a lamp on and Kareema was sitting on my side of the bed wearing a robe.

"Why you got that robe on?" I asked.

She rolled her eyes. "I was wondering if you were okay, but I see you are."

Bending over to kiss her, I smiled. "I'm good. Just a crazy-ass dream. Get naked and get back in this bed. I need you on top of me ASAP."

A minute or so later, the room was dark again, and I was on my back with her warm body on mine, drifting off to sleep until I heard her say, "Who is Omar?"

I didn't—*couldn't*—answer, so she kept talking. "You didn't hit me, but you were fucking Omar up. If I'd been in your line of fire,

I'd probably be in the emergency room right now."

I squeezed my already-shut eyes tightly. "I'ont wanna talk about that right now. Go to sleep, Kareema."

She tried to move from my body, but I held her there. "Omar is my father. I...he made us call him Omar most of the time. He used to fight me, snatch me out of my sleep and just go to waling on my ass from the time I was like eight. Said he was making me into a man. He kept doing that shit until I was old enough to kick his ass."

"Set, I'm—"

"It's all good. Just...let's go to sleep, baby."

"Okay."

6

Kareema

Now...

"The fuck wrong with you?" his clueless ass asked, as I stared out the passenger window. Las Vegas at night? The strip? It was everything, but I was too pissed to fully enjoy it. I hadn't even been there a full twenty-four hours and he'd managed to do something he'd never done before—piss me completely off.

"You mad about me fucking you with ole girl on the phone?"

I rolled my eyes. "If you know why I'm mad, why'd you ask?"

"Because I was hoping that wasn't it. You scared of her or something?"

"No! I just don't want her in my business! I said your name!"

"You coulda stopped me."

I snatched my head around to look at his silly, handsome-ass face. "How, Set?"

"Shit, if you'd told me to stop, I woulda stopped. I ain't a complete damn savage."

"And how in theeee fuck was I supposed to

tell you to stop while your dick was inside me, huh? How?"

His stupid ass grinned. "You ashamed of me, Kareema?"

I turned my whole body to face him. "Are you ashamed of me? Which of your friends know about us?"

Shaking his head, he mumbled, "You too pretty to be this petty."

"Yeah, that's what I thought, and where the fuck are you taking me?"

"Can't tell you. I'm tryna surprise your angry ass."

"Humph."

When we made it to the MGM Grand and he informed me that we were there for the Janet Jackson show, I tucked my tail and shut my mouth, and once we were back at his gorgeous apartment, I tried to think of ways to apologize for acting so childish. Shit, I loved the man and honestly didn't care who knew about us, but I wasn't spreading news he wasn't spreading. Nothing about our arrangement had changed except how I felt about him, and if I had any sense, I would end things before my heart got broken. Instead, after we'd walked into his place in silence and he'd informed me that he was taking a shower, I sat in his bedroom and waited until I heard him turn the water on. Then I shed my clothes and knocked on the shower door.

Sticking his head out the shower, he asked, "You need something?"

"Yeah…I'm sorry for acting like I acted earlier."

He shrugged. "It's all good, baby."

"Um, can I come in there with you?"

With a smile, he opened the door wider for me to join him, and as soon as I stepped inside the huge space, I dropped to a squat and took his wet dick into my mouth.

"Oh, shit! Ffffffffffuck!" he shouted, his voice a mixture of surprise and elation.

As I sucked, my head bobbing back and forth, he gripped the back of my head, stumbling a little, and soon, he was controlling the rhythm of me pleasing him, thrusting in and out of my mouth, *fucking* my mouth, groaning, his long, thick shaft hitting the back of my throat and making me gag as my eyes watered.

And I loved it.

I loved his moans, loved the way he was losing control, loved pleasing him. All of that made my pussy cream and throb. I swear I was about to climax.

After he pressed my head against his pelvis and dumped his load down my throat, I let him slip from my mouth and smiled up at him as his chest rapidly rose and fell. It wasn't the first time I'd sucked his dick, but it'd never been that intense before, and the next thing I knew, he was snatching me to my feet and kissing me like his life depended on it. Then, as the warm water battered our bodies, he held my face in his hands and asked, "What the fuck are you doing to me, Kareema?"

"The same thing you're doing to me, Set," I replied.

"How you gonna start fucking in the middle of our conversation? I mean, I'm sitting there telling you about this trifling nigga I need to put out my house and you start fucking?!" It was early the next morning, and I was sitting out on Set's balcony sure that the whole damn city could hear loud-ass Tricia through the phone.

"*He* started fucking *me*. What was I supposed to do? Stop him? Girl, sorry—not sorry, but that wasn't happening."

"The dick that good?"

"Yep."

"Shit!"

"Mm-hmm."

"No wonder you're keeping his ass a secret."

Glancing back to be sure Set was nowhere around, I softly said, "It's Set Mitchell."

"Huh?"

"My…" Shit, what was he to me? "I've been seeing Set Mitchell."

"Set Mitchell?! Crazy, fighting-ass Set Mitchell?!"

I rolled my eyes. "You gotta describe him like that? See, this is why I didn't tell you."

"Hell, that's how I know him from school!"

"Are you the person you were in high school, Trish?"

"No...so he's different?"

"Of course he is! He's forty-one just like me and you!"

"Wow! Never in a million years did I think it was him. Shit, I bet that *is* some good dick. When did y'all first hook up?"

"At our twenty-year class reunion."

"Ohhhh, no wonder you weren't mad about me not showing up."

"Yeah, well, even though it was foul of you to ghost me just to stay home and screw your man, you actually did me a favor. So there was no need for me to be mad."

"This is wild! So, he's nice to you?"

"Yeah, he's sweet to me...sweet and nasty."

"So, y'all are *together* together?"

"Oh, no. We're just hooking up, having fun. This shit ain't going nowhere."

Those words had barely left my mouth when I felt his energy. He was standing behind me on the balcony.

Set

"Why you so quiet?" she asked.

I shrugged, stabbed some fried potatoes with my fork, and shoved them in my mouth.

With a grin, she said, "You sad because I'm leaving tonight?"

I shrugged again. I was fucking pissed off about the shit I overheard her saying to whoever she was on the phone with, probably Tricia's talking ass. I remembered her from school, and she had a mouth on her back then, too. Anyway, she'd said this "shit" wasn't going nowhere, so it was like I knew it was. I wasn't good enough to be more than a good time for her. That shit hurt my damn feelings and instead of my grown ass saying that, I refused to speak at all.

"Hell, I'm sad too. I don't wanna go," she admitted, and when I glanced up at her and saw the look in her eyes, like she hadn't meant to say it but definitely meant what she said, my damn heart skipped a beat.

"Then don't go," I said. "Stay."

She stared at me, and I kept my eyes locked on her. I swear, minutes passed before she said, "Let me call and let someone know I won't be working tomorrow."

"Take the week off," jumped out of my mouth on its own.

She stared at me again before finally saying, "Okay."

7

Set

Two years earlier…

"Well, did you give him his medicine? You have to follow the directions for the ibuprofen, Tori. What? Did you crack the window or wipe him down with alcohol like I told you? Tori, we already took him to the doctor. He's not going to get better overnight…okay, I'll check on y'all later." Kareema ended the call and sighed, placing her phone on the nightstand and falling back in bed beside me.

"Everything okay?" I asked.

"Shit, I hope so."

"She wants you to come home?"

"She didn't outright ask me to, but I know she does."

"You wanna go back?"

"Honestly, I *should* want to, but I don't. I need her to…I think I messed her up. She just can't get this adulting thing down. She depends on me too much."

"Nah, I doubt that's your fault. You're too smart, always been. That's her daddy in her."

She turned and looked at me. "That *really*

makes it my fault. I picked his stupid ass to make a baby with. Then I scrambled to marry him because I was a good girl and embarrassed about being pregnant out of wedlock. Just young and dumb, struggled for years because he thought it was a privilege for him to make me his wife. Him working? That was optional."

"Nah, you were in love. Love makes you do some crazy shit, Kareema."

With raised eyebrows, she asked, "Set Jr.'s mom?"

"Oh, naw. I wasn't in love with her ass, just got caught slipping. I ain't mad, though. He's a good kid, real smart."

"He's at Grambling, right?"

"Yeah. But uh…I ain't fall in love until I was old as hell."

"Really? What happened? Why'd y'all break up?"

My grown ass should've told her I was referring to her, that I was making up trips just to be in her presence, hear her voice, see her face, touch her soft skin, and get a taste of her addictive pussy, but instead, I kissed her, pulled her on top of me, and said, "Enough talking. You know what to do."

She grinned down at me as she reached between us and grabbed my hard dick. "I sure do."

Kareema

Now…

"Thanks, Yolanda…oh, you'll do fine, and you can always call me if you need to…all right, see you next week." I ended the call to find Set's eyes on me as we sat in his living room that Sunday afternoon.

"Everything good?" he asked.

"Yep. Got one of my best teachers in charge while I'm gone. Now, let me call Tori so she won't be worried when I don't show up on Monday."

He nodded and then moved from his seat across from me and squeezed his big body next to mine on the love seat, wrapping an arm around my shoulder.

A few seconds later, I was enduring my daughter's whining in response to me informing her that Yolanda would be in charge in my absence. "I should be in charge," she advised me.

"You're not qualified, Tori," I replied.

"I'm your daughter!"

"Yes, you are, but that's not a qualification. Yolanda has more experience than you. You can't handle all that responsibility."

"Wow…woooooooow. Okay, fine. Whatever, Mom."

"Bye, sweetie."

"Bye!"

I guessed she was pissed.

Whatever.

I leaned forward and laid my phone on the coffee table, turned to look at Set, and was instantly crowded by his scent, his body heat, and then his mouth met mine. He kissed me deeply, pulling me onto his lap and gripping my barely-there ass. You'd think I had an hourglass figure the way Set acted.

We were both half naked, so it didn't take much effort for my breast to end up in his mouth or my hand to end up around his dick. Soon, we were both moaning and whimpering our way to climax, and he wasn't even inside me.

"Shit, Kareema. I can't get enough of you," he murmured.

I threw my head back as he found my clit and stroked it. "Set…"

"I could taste you every damn day, be inside you every damn hour."

"Oh!" I whined, an orgasm assaulting me as I squirted all over his lap. A few seconds later, he'd exploded in my hand with a roar against my breast.

After catching my breath, I peered down between us. "We made a mess."

After he kissed me, he hummed, "Mm-hmm."

*****

"You gonna feed me?" I asked from my spot lying on top of him on his sofa.

"Yeah, you wanna go out?"

"We can, but you'll have to let me get up."

"Then we'll order in."

I laughed. "Weird ass."

"Did I tell you your girl, Trish, sent me a friend request?"

Lifting my head from his chest, I said, "No, you didn't. Did you accept it?"

"Am I supposed to?"

"If you want to."

My phone buzzed on the coffee table, and I squinted to see the screen.

Tori.

Shit.

I should've ignored it but slid off Set's body, making him groan in protest, and grabbed my phone.

He sat up on the sofa giving me room to sit beside him as I answered my daughter's call with, "Hello?"

"What the fuck is wrong with you?!" was screamed into my ear.

It wasn't Tori; it was her stupid-ass father.

"Who the fuck is that?" Set asked rather loudly. I supposed he could hear Shawn through the phone.

"Who the fuck asking who I am?!" Shawn shrieked.

I wasn't sure who to answer but opted for my ex. "Shawn? What are you doing with Tori's phone?"

"She came over here crying about you firing her! Why you do that?"

Set stood and left the living room without a word.

"Shawn, I didn't fire her, and even if I did, that would be between me and her."

"She's my got-damn daughter, too!"

"Oh, you want to be a father now that she's damn grown? Nigga, please." I hung up on his ass and went on a search for Set, finding him in his bedroom staring out the window.

Before I could speak, he said, "So you got that motherfucker in your phone under your daughter's name, Kareema? All this time, I thought you were talking to your daughter and you been talking to another nigga while you were in the bed with me? I know you ain't really mine, but shit! I don't deserve no respect?"

My mouth dropped open, because...the fuck? "What?!" I responded.

"You heard me!" he thundered.

Placing my hands on my hips, I asked, "Set,

have you heard his voice on my phone before? Ever?"

Nothing from him.

"You seriously think I've been pretending to talk to Tori but have actually been talking to his sorry ass all this time? I don't believe this shit."

He finally turned to look at me, the anger in his eyes reminding me of his younger self. "What you want to eat?" he barked.

"Huh?"

"You said you was hungry. What you wanna eat?"

"So we're done talking about Shawn?"

"Yeah."

I sighed my frustration. "It doesn't matter. I'll eat whatever. You know I'm not picky."

"A'ight."

About an hour later, as we silently ate pizza, he said, "I'm sorry about earlier. It was fucked up for me to accuse you of that shit. You a good girl, always have been."

I raised my eyes to meet his. "It's all good, Set."

He chuckled and continued eating.

8

Kareema

"Wow, this place is nice…and huge," I said, as he led me through the pristine glass entry doors of Mitchell Fitness.

Inside, it looked like any other gym — workout equipment, mirrors, people exercising, but this was *Set's* gym. The man I loved owned his own gym and had clients that he trained. That was why we were there. He had a couple of clients to see and didn't want to leave me at his place alone, and truth be told, I didn't want to be away from him anyway. Shit, if I could've glued myself to his fine ass, I would've.

"Let me give you a tour," he offered, taking my hand in his.

"Okay, but I don't have to work out, do I? I'm allergic to exercise."

He chuckled. "Come on, now…you expect me to believe you got this fine with no exercise?"

I shook my head. "Whatever, Set."

If I thought I was proud of him because of my initial view of his gym, I was damn near in tears when he showed me the room that held the boxing ring. There were boxing bags in the corners of the room, and the walls were covered with paintings of Set, replicas of the boxing photos I'd seen of him on social media and in his home. My breath got caught somewhere between my lungs and my mouth as I slowly did a three-sixty, taking it all in.

"So, what do you think?" he asked, with a look on his face that told me he really wanted to know.

I dropped my eyes, because I was literally on the verge of tears, and softly said, "Set, it's…" Words actually escaped me. I didn't know how to verbalize the pride that was bubbling inside of me, so I reached up to grasp the face of this man who was a foot taller than me, and kissed him, hoping what I was feeling would somehow be transferred to him.

When the kiss ended, he smiled. "So…you like it?"

Through a giggle, I replied, "I do. I love it, Set. I'm…I'm so proud of you."

Cradling my face in his hands, he returned, "That means a lot coming from you, Kareema. A whole lot."

All I could do was fall into him and hug him tightly, and he hugged me right back. We parted when two men filed into the room and spoke to Set who quickly herded me out into the hallway.

"You're not going to introduce me to your

friends?"

"They're actually my employees, and hell no. Them niggas always tryna fuck somebody."

It's a damn shame how giddy those words made me feel.

I explored the gym alone while Set worked with his first client of the day, an older lady who was in way better shape than me. If I hadn't been wearing a sundress and sandals, her level of fitness might have influenced me to hop on a treadmill.

That session was followed by his second and last client of the day, a much younger woman, a very friendly, very flirtatious younger woman with slim hips and huge breasts. She was basically a younger version of me, and the way she kept giggling and touching his huge right bicep made me perch myself on a weight bench a few feet from them and watch with narrowed eyes as Set's ass laughed right along with her. They sure in the hell looked like more than trainer and client to me. They looked like they were fucking, and even though I had no right to be, I was steaming by the time that big-tittied heifer left and Set strolled his ass over to me. He smiled down at me until he noticed the uncontrollable scowl I was wearing.

"The fuck is wrong with you now?" he asked.

With a shrug, I retorted, "Nothing. You're single and free to do what you want."

"The fuck does that mean?"

"It means…nothing, Set. Absolutely nothing."

He kept his eyes affixed to me for a few moments, and then that smile returned to his face. "You jealous of Lizzie?"

I rolled my eyes. "That can't be her real name. Who the hell names their black child Lizzie?"

He laughed. "Stand up. I wanna show you something."

"What? Lizzie's sweat or something?"

More laughing from his ass, and then, "No, not that."

"Another tour? I've seen everything, Set."

He backed up a little. "You ain't seen this. Stand up, Kareema."

With a pout, I stood from the bench and watched as he dropped to the floor, the muscles of his back rippling as he fell into a push-up.

Before I could ask him why he was doing a damn push-up, he said, "Lay on my back."

"Huh?"

"You heard me. Lie down on my back, Kareema."

"Now? Here?"

"Yeah. When and where else?"

Through a sigh, I lay on his back and wrapped my arms around him when he told me to hold on. Then he did another push-up with me on his back, and a giggle escaped my mouth. He kept moving up and down, reminding me of him being between my legs, which made my pussy liquify as I held on and grinned like a fool. Some of the gym's patrons moved closer, surrounding us, and when he was done and we were both on our feet, they applauded, a sound that surrounded us as Set leaned in and kissed me.

"You still mad?" he asked.

"I wasn't mad anyway," I lied.

He grabbed my hand. "Uh-huh."

Set

Eighteen months earlier…

"You never told me how you met husband number two," I said, as she lay next to me looking as exhausted as I felt. We'd been at it all day, filling this hotel room in San Antonio with moans and whimpers and shit.

Her eyes were closed as she answered me through a yawn. "You never asked, but I met him when he came to pick his granddaughter up from my day care one afternoon when I wasn't hiding out in my office."

"Granddaughter? You married an old muhfucker?"

She opened her eyes and gave me a smirk. "Really?"

"I'm just saying…"

"I was thirty when we got married. He was fifty-six."

"Word?"

"Yep. We were married for three years before he passed away, best three years of my life. I'll never find another him."

"What was his name? I know you told me before, but I forgot."

"Vincent. Vincent Wise."

"Why you ain't keep his name?"

"Hurt too bad at first. So I took my maiden name back."

"You really loved him, huh?"

"I…I appreciated him for caring about me and treating me so good, and yes, I loved him. Vincent and I didn't share a lot of passion, but we were good together."

"Y'all didn't fuck?"

"I didn't say that. Of course, we did."

"But not like you and me fuck?"

"No…nothing has ever been quite like you and me."

"Yeah, I feel you on that. Uh, Kareema?"

"Yeah?"

"You still don't wanna get married again?"

"Sure don't. How about you? Still no plans of ever getting married?"

"Nope, no plans at all."

9

Kareema

Now…

After the gym, we had lunch at a Chinese restaurant and were now in Set's bed, still clothed but with our mouths fused. His big hand was on the side of my face as we kissed and kissed and kissed. I'd forgotten how nice it felt just to kiss, no other stimulation, but at the same time, *all* of the stimulation. We were silent, no moans or whimpers or groans, no sense of urgency, just this moment and this feeling that we shared, this…adoration.

This *love*.

Well, if this *wasn't* love then maybe I had no idea what love was. I knew I loved him, and he at least acted like he loved me.

You should tell him. Tell him you love him.

Hell naw! I'm not putting myself out there like that only to find out this man has another woman, a secret wife, anything that could and would break my damn heart. Shit no!

I had no idea where any of those thoughts came from, but they made me lose my tongue rhythm, and Set noticed it.

After ending the kiss, he opened those pretty eyes of his and fixed them on me. "What's wrong?"

"Nothing," I lied.

He grinned. "You lying your ass off. What you wanna do tonight?"

"This. I wanna lie here and kiss you all night long."

He lifted an eyebrow. "For real?"

"Mm-hmm."

"You don't want me to hit it from the back after I eat it from the back? You don't want me to put your legs behind your head and make you squirt all over the damn place? You don't wanna ride this muhfuckin' pogo stick until you start screaming and shit while I got your titty in my mouth?"

I laughed. "First of all, pogo stick? Why are you so damn silly?"

He shrugged while wearing a boyish grin.

"Second," I continued, "I told you I ain't riding you no more. It's insulting the way you don't even raise your head to suck my titties. Makes me feel like they're long. I'm getting a breast reduction."

"I'll be damned if you do! You ain't touching those fucking masterpieces. I'll lose my shit if you do that. I *need* those titties."

"Whatever. I still ain't riding you ever again."

So about ten minutes later, I found myself sliding up and down Set's dick like a damn fool, howling as he thrusted upward, hitting my cervix and making me rain juices all over him. At one point, as I reached behind me and gripped his thighs, my hand kept slipping, so I had to plant my feet on the bed and grip the sides of his hard stomach, soon finding myself on my knees again as Set frowned up at me and grabbed the back of my head, snatching it down to his face so he could capture my mouth.

After he let my head go, his savage ass flipped me over onto my back and was between my legs and inside me in damn near one move. Resting on his elbows, he rolled into me while staring into my eyes. "I love this pussy, Kareema. You can't give this pussy to no one else, you hear me? No…one…else. This...my...pussy!" He accented each word with a thrust that made my coochie quiver.

"Set…oh, shit! Set!"

We went on like that, screaming as the sound of him plowing into my pussy and the scent of our bodies mating filled his bedroom. When a deep "V" formed in his brow and he started groaning, "KareemaKareemaKareema-KareemaKareema!" I knew he was about to meet his happy ending. He always sounded so tortured, like it hurt and pleased him to come. It made me feel powerful as hell for this man to unravel like that while inside of me, for him to unravel like that *because* he was inside of me.

Yeah, moments like this made me believe Captain Marvel didn't have shit on the strength of my pussy.

After he emptied inside of me, he rolled off my body onto his stomach and grunted, "Get on my back, baby."

So I did.

Set

"Set, you're still up?" she asked, her voice heavy with sleep. My bedside clock told me it was three in the morning, and I hadn't slept at all.

"Yeah," I said.

"What's wrong? Can't sleep?"

"I don't wanna sleep."

A lamp popped on, and she was frowning as she inspected my face. "Why? You been having nightmares again?"

I shook my head. "No, baby."

"Then what's going on?"

"Nothing. I was just…I…I was watching you sleep. I wanted to watch you sleep."

"Oh, okay. So you're good?"

"Yeah."

"Good." She smiled and turned the lamp off. Then she snuggled close to me, soon drifting back off to sleep.

That was why I loved her ass so much, enough to fuck up the world for her if I had to. No matter how weird she might've thought my damaged ass was, she never let it push her away from me. She never stopped seeing me or giving herself to me.

At that moment, I was convinced this woman was created just for me.

10

Kareema

"My father…he was always good to my mom, treated her like a queen, and I really think he believed he was making men out of me and Shu and Jah. Fighting us, making us build decks and shit. Sometimes, he'd make us rake leaves then he'd dump them out of the trash bags and make us rake them again. One time, he got us up out of bed at like two in the morning and made us paint the damn living room, and we had school the next day. I can't tell you how many times he'd make us fight each other, how often he'd just walk up to me and punch me in the chest and dare me to cry. I was like, ten damn years old!

"Anyway, my mom wasn't allowed to hug us. She told me he would only let her hold us if she was feeding us when we were babies. That was it. And him? Wasn't no hugging or patting us on the back. None of that, because he was raising men. Men didn't need hugs or kisses. Men, especially black men, needed to be ready for a fucked-up world that didn't have nothing for them but hard knocks and injustice."

We were eating breakfast in his bed the morning before I was to leave when, out of the blue, he started talking about his past, his abusive-ass father who I wanted to shoot in the damn neck, and his obviously weak mother.

"He made me good at fighting, though. Shit, I had no choice but to be good at it," he continued. "In a way, he gave me my first career which lcd to me opening up my gym."

I didn't know what to say and honestly believed he was talking more to himself than to me at that point, so I remained silent.

"I still fight," he said.

I frowned at him, but before I could say a word, he kept talking. "Underground shit, not official fighting. I don't do it often, but sometimes, I don't know, shit from when I was a kid starts fucking with me and I just need to hit a motherfucker to make it stop. But when I'm with you and for a long time after I get to see you? I don't feel none of that." He had been staring down at his empty plate but was now staring at me.

"Set—"

"Thank you for that."

"For what?"

"For being you."

"Oh. Well, thank you for being *you*, Set Mitchell. I...I feel the same way. When we're together, I don't feel like a shitty mother or a fool who married an asshole or a woman with the bad luck of her one good husband dying."

"You ain't none of that anyway, Kareema. You…you're perfect."

I smiled. "Thank you, Set. I'm glad you think so."

"You're welcome, baby, and I don't think shit. I *know* it."

All I could do was lean in and kiss him.

And he kissed me right back.

*****

Set

I watched her get in that TSA line and wanted to fucking scream. Okay, so the truth is that my six-foot-one, two hundred and fifty-pound, muscled-up ass wanted to cry, because she was leaving me to face my got-damn demons alone. I was tired of facing that shit alone.

I needed a lot of stuff—counseling, therapy, group therapy. Hell, I probably needed shock therapy, but more than any of that, I needed to tell Kareema how I felt and what I wanted—her.

I just wanted her. That was it. I wasn't fucked up about anything else. Yeah, I had my son and we got along well enough. We weren't super close, because I was scared I'd be the kind of father my pops was, so I kept a safe distance from him while still trying to show him I loved him. I didn't think he hated me, but I also didn't think he'd award me father of the year and I was okay with that. What haunted me was the idea of being without Kareema. What if she got tired of my ass and found someone with the balls to commit to her even though she said she didn't want that? Hell, I'd probably still be tongue-tied and rather than telling her how I felt about her, I'd most likely do some stupid shit like kill the nigga to get him out of my way and still not tell her how I felt, because I was just fucked all the way up. But more than being fucked up, I was scared, petrified that I'd tell her I loved her and she'd fucking laugh at me. But I knew she wouldn't do that. She wasn't cruel, but I just wasn't sure how she'd react. Would she love me back?

Hell, no. Why would she love my screwed-up ass? I doubted if my own damn mama loved me. I couldn't expect Kareema to love me, could I?

I loved her, though. I loved the shit out of her.

I really did.

11

Kareema

A week after I returned home from Las Vegas, I found myself sitting in my office, which had taken on the characteristics of a jail cell to me. Owning my own daycare center was never a dream for me. My business was born out of necessity. Shawn's sorry ass couldn't keep a job and we had bills to pay. Our broke asses stayed with my mom the first few months of our marriage, but then she died from an aneurysm that my young, clueless ass probably caused, and shit just went from bad to worse. I didn't have time to mourn her. As her only child, I had to plan her funeral, and after she was buried, I had to figure out how to keep the lights on and feed my newborn daughter. Since I had no education other than a high school diploma, I started keeping kids. Before I knew it, I had a good little gig going on and finally woke up and got rid of Shawn before Tori was old enough to go to school. My business grew enough for me to have the garage in the house I'd inherited from my mom converted into a small daycare, and now, more than twenty years later, Kinder Kuties was a thriving business with ten classrooms housed in a renovated community center complete with a playground and indoor basketball court, and I was responsible for all of it. I'd always been responsible for every damn thing except when I was with Vincent. At least he paid the utilities and bought me gifts. Did I really love him? Not in the way a wife was supposed to love her husband, because after Shawn, I vowed to never marry for love again. I was convinced no good came of love. Vincent felt more like a friend I shared a home with and occasionally had some decent sex with, but I was thankful for that. It was better than the good sex and frustration I'd had with Shawn.

Anyway, I still lived in my mom's house, had no mortgage, drove a nice car, and made a great living. By all definitions of the word, I was successful, but truth be told, at that moment, I wished I was perched on a weight bench getting heated about one of Set's clients being too damn friendly with him. I was over being alone.

I let my eyes drop to my phone, to the text he'd sent just minutes earlier: *I miss you.*

In response, I sent back: *I miss you too.*

*****

"What do you mean you're not coming to work today? Tori, you don't sound sick," I said, as I gripped my forehead.

"I'm not sick, but I think me and Monté broke up last night."

"You think?"

"Yeah, and I know it's because Yolanda been in his ear! She can't stand to see us happy just because she's got a baby with him! I'm not coming back to work until you fire her!" my only child screamed into the phone.

"First of all, you better lower your voice and recognize who the hell you're talking to right now. Second, that negro ain't shit. He doesn't even have a damn job, and it makes no sense for you to lose yours over him!"

"Lose mine?! So you're firing me? Really, Mama? You're choosing her over me?"

"No, girl! I'm choosing my business over some foolishness! You are an adult, Tori, and you have a child to take care of. I gave you a damn job so you can do just that. You owe it to yourself and him to put on your big girl panties and bring your ass to work. Now!"

I hung up and called a couple of retired teachers I kept on standby as potential substitutes, because I knew my daughter well enough to know she actually wasn't coming to work. Luckily, I was able to get one of them to come in, and I had to watch Tori's class along with her assistant until the sub arrived. Then I closed myself up in my office and rubbed my now throbbing head and closed my eyes. I was digging in my purse for pain reliever when my cell rang—Set.

I sat there and stared at my phone, because Set never called me. He was a text person. So the phone had stopped ringing before I got over the shock and picked it up. I called him back and damn near cried when I heard that sexy growl of his. "Hello? Kareema?"

"Yeah. Hey, Set."

"Hey. I, uh…how you doing?"

"Okay. You?"

"I don't know. Look, my dad always said only simps talk about feelings and shit, but it's some stuff I need to say to you."

"Okay, I'm listening," I said, tears filling my eyes at the apparent vulnerability in his voice.

"A'ight, so look—"

My office door flew open, slamming against the wall and making me yelp.

"The fuck was that?!" Set yelled in my ear.

"Shawn?!" I squeaked. "Why the hell did you just bust in my office?" I looked around him to see Damiana, my receptionist, looking bewildered and knew he'd stormed right past her and busted in on me. I also knew this was about our spoiled-ass daughter.

"Get off the damn phone," Shawn barked, stalking over to me and snatching it from my ear. I watched as he threw it against a wall and my blood began to boil.

"Damiana, call the police!" I ordered and watched as she scurried back to her desk.

Shawn slammed my office door shut and stared down at where I hadn't moved from my chair, shaking his head at me. "You know what? I always knew you were slow, but I thought I could trust you to take care of Tori. I thought you was a halfway decent mother, but you just keep fucking with her over some raggedy bitch you got working here, got her coming to my house crying and shit, and you know I can't stand to see her cry."

"You know your daughter lies, right? Oh yeah…you don't, do you? You two only started having a relationship when she got grown and started forcing herself into your life, making it impossible for you to keep ignoring her. Now you wanna play big bad daddy to a grown ass woman who keeps running to you like she's five because I won't let her have her way? Get the hell out of here before the police arrive. I know you've got to have warrants. So go home to your latest benefactor and tell Tori if she wants her job, she needs to bring her ass to work!"

He glared at me before muttering, "This ain't over," and snatching my door open. He'd been gone for about ten minutes before I thought to locate my phone and was thankful that the expensive-ass case I had it in had protected it. I tried to call Set back but got no answer, so I turned the police away when they arrived and spent the rest of the day holed up in my office trying not to cry.

Set

"There he is! I told you his ass be hanging over here."

I couldn't answer my brother or look at him. I had tunnel vision like a motherfucker.

"Set, you sure about this? You look like you about to kill the nigga. Maybe you should calm down first. You just hopped off a plane."

"Naw, Jah. This can't wait. That motherfuck— you coming or what?"

"I ain't letting your ass go over there alone."

"A'ight, let's go then."

I jumped out the driver's seat of my rental and with my baby brother on my heels, walked across the street to the Bauman Courts. I'd spent a lot of time shooting hoops and getting in fights there back in the day. Now it seemed that the only folks hanging out there were grown niggas who didn't have shit to do. This nigga was sitting on the trunk of a car, probably his woman's car, and I stepped right up to the crowd of him and four other fools, my eyes glued to this motherfucker who kept putting way too much bass in his voice when he talked to Kareema.

"Aw, shit! It's two of the Mitchell boys! I'd know y'all chinky-eyed muhfuckas anywhere! What's up, fellas?" Shawn Thomas said, holding a fist out to me.

I didn't say a word or bump his ashy-ass fist. I just glared at him.

"Aye, y'all other niggas need to step. Set need to handle some business with Thomas," Jah's huge ass said.

With no questions asked, the other dudes scrambled to leave.

"I ain't got no business with neither one of y'all so I'ma just leave, too," Shawn said, eyes on the ground and hands raised.

I shook my head. "Nah, nigga...you stay here. We got some shit to clear up."

"Some shit to clear up? What shit?" He looked like he was ready to climb over the roof of the car, anything to get away from me and Jah.

"Shit like why you think you can fuck with Kareema the way you been fucking with her."

"Kareema? What the fuck? What she got to do with anything? The hell are you talking about?!"

"I'm talking about me being on the phone with her earlier today and you busting in her office on her."

"On the phone with her? You fucking Kareema?"

"Stay the fuck away from her, Thomas, or I'ma make good on the ass-kicking I promised you back in the day," I said, ignoring his stupid-ass question. Obviously, I was fucking her.

I'd turned to leave when I heard the familiar sound of a bone cracking and turned to see Shawn Thomas slide from the trunk of the car onto the ground, blood oozing from his nose.

"Shit, I hurt my damn hand hitting that Cro-Magnon head-ass nigga," Jah said.

I rubbed the back of my neck. "Damn, Jah. I didn't tell you to hit him. That's Kareema's daughter's father, man."

Jah shrugged. "He been fucking with your girl. I know how you feel about her. So you don't owe me nothing."

This damn fool...

12

Kareema

"Set?! What are you doing here?" I shrieked.

"I sent him a DM letting him know about your car," Trish said, making me regret calling her for a ride when I left work late to find all four of my tires slashed. Not that I wasn't glad to see Set and—

"Jah Mitchell? Wow!" I shouted upon seeing Set's big little brother step into my living room behind him.

"'Sup, Kareema," Jah greeted me with a wide grin. He moved to hug me, but Set blocked him and muttered, "Hell naw, nigga. Back your big ass up."

Jah raised his hands. "My bad, man. Just being friendly."

"I ain't see no message," Set said. "What happened to her car?"

As Trish gleefully told all my damn business to Set like I'd declared him my man to her rather than a frequent fuck buddy, I resumed the posture I'd taken before he entered my house, slumped on the sofa with my head in my hands.

I jumped when I felt someone sit next to me and opened my eyes to see that it was Set with so much concern in his eyes that I *had* to cry.

Pulling me to him, he softly said, "I got you. I'll fuck up whoever did this. I promise you that. I will fuck them all the way up. On sight. I will put my foot—"

Shaking my head, I looked up at him with a wet face. "You can't do that. It was my daughter."

Set

I kept holding her, my eyes sweeping the neat living room of her house before I finally said, "How you know for sure? You saw her?"

"She called in sick today, but I saw her and her supposed-to-be ex-man pulling off the lot at my daycare this evening. Even if it was him and not her, she was there and didn't stop him. I gave her so much trying to make up for Shawn not being there and I just ruined her and now she hates me."

"I told you she's the way she is because of her father, not you. It's genetics."

"And I told you I picked the fool to procreate with. It's definitely on me."

"You were a kid. Stop being so hard on

yourself."

We both fell silent, and then I realized Jah and Tricia were still in the room, both of them staring at us.

"Damn, this is sweet, seeing Set all in love and shit. I mean, I already knew you were all in for her the way you got my ass driving by here checking on her house at night like a damn security guard. Then you flew your ass here today to—"

"Jah, I'm good. You can go on home. I'll get at you in the morning," I said, interrupting my brother.

"Nigga, you drove. My car at the crib," he replied.

"I can run him home for you, Set. I need to be heading to my place anyway. That's if you're good, Kareema. I can stay if you need me to, but it looks like you're in good hands," Tricia said.

"I'm fine. Thanks for the ride home. I'll call you tomorrow," Kareema told her friend.

"Sounds like a plan, then. Shit, I remember you, too, but you done thickened up, ain't you? I like them braids you got," Jah said, trying to shoot his shot at Tricia.

In response, Tricia rolled her eyes. "I got a man, and if I didn't have one, I wouldn't let your giant ass break my pussy."

As Jah followed her out the door, he rubbed his hands together. "So you heard about me, huh?" he asked, and then he started doing some frat call.

Tricia's distant voice replied, "Boy, get your ass on in this car," as Jah shut the front door behind them. Then I watched Kareema lift from the couch to lock it.

Turning to look at me, she asked, "You've been having your brother watch my house? Why?"

I sighed. Jah and his big-ass mouth. With a shrug, I replied, "I'ont know. Because this city is fucked up. Every other day somebody getting shot. I was...I was worried about you."

"You told him about us?"

"Yeah."

"Set—"

"We can talk more later. I know you got to be tired, and that flight kicked my ass. You got an alarm system, or are you coming to a hotel with me?"

She frowned. "You're not staying here?"

"Didn't think you'd want me to."

"Well, I don't feel like leaving and I...I want you to stay.

"A'ight. Then I'll stay."

13

Kareema

"Set?" My voice penetrated the darkness. I wasn't sure if he was awake but figured he was.

"Yeah, baby?" he responded, making my pussy purr. I almost forgot what I wanted to ask.

"How long has your brother been checking on me?"

There was a moment of silence before he said, "Um…about a year, I think. At least I been paying him to do it that long."

"Paying him?"

"Yeah…"

"Why didn't you tell me you had him doing that?"

"I don't know. I guess I thought it would make you feel uncomfortable."

"Oh…"

"Does it? I mean, I ain't on no stalker shit."

"I know. I'm…thank you for looking out for me."

"It's nothing, baby."

"Why'd you come here if it wasn't because of Tricia's message?"

He groaned, "Kareema, go to sleep. I ain't tryna do all this talking right now."

I didn't respond, and I guess that was response enough, because he sighed, and said, "Because a motherfucker busted in your office while I was talking to you on the got-damn phone and I wanted to make sure you were okay."

"What were you trying to tell me on the phone?"

"I ain't ready to talk about that no more. Your ex fucked up the moment."

"Set—"

"Baby, *go to sleep*."

"I can't. You love me, Set?"

Silence.

"Do you?"

"Do you love me, Kareema?"

Silence from me.

"Do you?" he parroted me.

I sighed and thought *fuck it*. "Yes."

"You do?" he asked, his voice somewhere in the rafters.

"Yes, Set…I do. I love you."

"Shit." His voice quivered.

"What?"

He sniffled. "I ain't think you loved me."

"Why?"

"Because I'm…I thought I wasn't good enough for you. I thought you still saw me like everyone else does."

I moved closer to him in the darkness, so close that his body heat surrounded me. I kissed him, felt his tears as they rolled onto our lips. "Set, you are a wonderful man, a little savage, but wonderful, successful, caring, protective, and that dick? That tongue? I will cut a bitch over them."

He chuckled.

"You're laughing, but I mean it."

"Kareema?"

"Yes?"

"How long have you loved me?"

"Probably since the first time you touched me. So, three years."

I felt him wipe his face. "Me, too. I've loved you that long, too."

"So you *do* love me?"

"With my whole fucking soul, Kareema."

"Who else did you tell about us?"

"Shu. Just Shu and Jah. I needed someone to know. I *had* to tell someone. You mad?"

"No. I'm…I'm flattered."

"Good."

"Set?"

"Yeah, baby?"

"I'm glad you love me."

"I'm glad you love me, too. Now lay on top of me."

With a smile, I said, "Okay."

Set

I woke up to voices, Kareema's and someone else's. The house wasn't all that big and she'd left the bedroom door open whenever she left the bed, so instead of getting up to see what was going on, I stayed in the bed and let my ears do the work. But when I heard her say her daughter's name, I threw on my sweats and a t-shirt and left the room, finding Kareema and her younger twin in the kitchen.

"Morning," I said.

Two heads shot in my direction. Kareema's concerned eyes softened when they fell on me. "Good morning. Set, this is my daughter, Tori. Tori, this is Set, the man I just told you about."

That shit made my heart skip like four beats. "'Sup, Tori? Good to meet you."

Tori turned to look at me, and her mouth dropped open. "Wow, I mean, good to meet you, too!" She turned and mouthed something to Kareema that made her giggle.

"And this is my grandson, Apollo," Kareema informed me.

I smiled at the sleeping little boy in her lap.

"Apollo, Greek god. I'm named after a god too. A fucked up one, but you know." I shrugged.

"Sit down and join us, Set. I made breakfast. I can fix you a plate," Kareema offered.

"I got it. I don't want you to wake the baby

up."

Breakfast was cool, and evidently, they'd worked shit out before I got in there, because they were being real friendly with each other. All I cared about was that Kareema seemed happy. That was all that mattered to me.

After Tori and Apollo left, I asked, "Y'all good?"

"Yeah. She apologized because her getaway driver told her to. Guess he had second thoughts after helping her vandalize my property. He's going to buy me a new set of tires. I'm not sure how, though, since he's unemployed." She sighed. "Anyway, she and him and his baby mama all sat down and talked last night, and all is well. Tori promised not to act up anymore."

"You believe her?"

"No, but I threatened to take custody of her son if she doesn't stop acting a damn fool. She's actually a good mother to him, now. It took her a while to get the hang of being a mother but she's good with him. Still, I'll take him if I feel like I need to."

"Where was he when she pulled that shit yesterday?"

"With his other grandmother. She's a good woman, spoils him more than I do."

"Where's his father?"

"In the pen. Drugs."

"Damn."

"Yeah. Set, she said someone beat her dad up. You know anything about that?"

"Word? Naw, I don't know shit about that."

"I know you're lying."

"Why I gotta be lying?"

All she did was smirk at me, and I smiled at her.

Shaking her head, she stood from the table and started gathering the breakfast dishes. I stood and grabbed the rest of the dishes, putting them in the sink and stopping her when she tried to go back to the table, turning her to face the kitchen counter and stepping behind her.

As I buried my face in her neck and reached around to squeeze both of her titties, she whimpered, "Set..."

"Hmm?" I asked, as I moved one hand from her titty and slid it into her pajama bottoms, finding her hot pussy and slipping a finger inside it. I moaned into her neck, my dick trying to drill a hole in my pants. "Your pussy feels so good, baby. I could play with this motherfucker all day."

"Uh!" she whined.

I slid my finger out of her pussy and stroked her clit, making her jerk. "You gonna come for me, Kareema?"

"Ohhhhh!"

"Come for me, baby. I want you to squirt all over my hand. I want this pussy soaking wet when I slide inside it."

"Set!"

I pressed my mouth to her ear as I stroked her clit faster. "Come, Kareema. Come, baby. Do it. Do it, baby. Come for me."

Her breathing was loud before it stopped altogether as she let out a hard grunt, and shouted, "Shhhhhhit!"

Then she made it rain all over my hand, and I snatched her pajamas down. "Bend over, baby," I growled.

She did, and I drilled my way inside that pussy of hers that always made me work for it. Once inside, my damn knees buckled a little, but I held it together, leaning over her back to ask her, "Whose pussy is this, Kareema?"

"Yours, baby!"

"Whose?"

"Yours, Set! Yours! Oh, shit, it's all yours!"

I fucked Kareema until sweat started dripping from my face to her back, not wanting it to end and wishing I could stay inside her until the end of time. I loved her so damn much it made my chest tight, so when that nut hit my ass and there was no turning back, I screamed, "I love you-I love you-I love you-I love you-I love youuuuuuu!"

"I-I-I love you, too!" she cried in response.

14

Kareema

"…and this is Tori's classroom when she's not calling in. She teaches the four-year-olds," I said, waving at Tori through the window on the door.

"Aw, now. You gotta believe in her more than that, baby," Set said.

"I know. I'm trying."

Tori opened the door with a smile and chirped, "Hey! You caught us eating our snacks. Say hello to Ms. Kareema and her friend, everyone!"

"Hi, Ms. Kareema," the kids chorused.

"Hey, everyone! This is my friend, Mr. Set," I replied.

"Hi, Mr. Set!" they sang.

"What's up, y'all?" Set greeted them with a grin.

"Ms. Kareema? Guess what I wanna be when I grow up!" a very talkative little girl named Ashton asked.

"What?" I said.

"I wanna be a rock so I can throw myself in the ocean!"

"Oh, wow! That's…interesting, sweetie," I replied.

Set softly muttered, "The fuck?"

"Ms. Kareema? Kaden said you having a baby," little Undray informed me.

Damn, I wasn't exactly skinny, but I didn't look pregnant, did I?

"Well, Kaden is mistaken. I'm not having a baby," I assured Undray.

Kaden hopped his little yellow self up and ran to me. "Uh-hunh! You having two babies! See? One, two!" he advised, as he pointed to my breasts.

"Kaden, go finish your cinnamon roll," I said, quickly shutting the door and leading a laughing Set down the hall.

"It wasn't that funny, negro," I hissed.

"Yeah it was! Damn, little man said *two* babies!" He stopped, doubling over and clutching his stomach.

"I can't stand your ass," I gritted, stomping away from him.

"Wait, I'm sorry. Show me the rest of the place." He was wiping tears from his eyes.

Rolling mine, I responded, "That's it. That's all there is to see if my little daycare."

"This ain't little, Kareema. It's nice, real nice, but I knew it would be. I knew you was about your business."

Grinning, I grasped his hand. "Thank you,

Set."

"You welcome, Ms. Two Babies."

"Ugh!"

More laughter from his overgrown ass.

Once in my office, he sat in the chair in front of my desk and slid down, opening his legs and propping his elbows on the arms as he watched me take my regular seat. "Hey, can we talk about something, baby?" he asked.

"Not if it involves my titties being babies."

He chuckled. "Naw, not that."

"What you wanna talk about, then? How you're about to eat my pussy in my office?"

He grinned and shook his head. "Freaky ass. But naw, I was just thinking you're probably gonna miss this place, huh?"

I frowned. "Why would I miss it?"

"Because you're leaving with me. Tomorrow."

"Huh? What are you talking about, Set? I'm not going anywhere."

"Yeah, you are. I ain't leaving you here in this fucked-up town. I can't take care of your ass like that. Only so much Jah can do. Shu works too much to take up his slack. So you gotta come with me."

"Set, I'm not leaving my business, my daughter, my grandson! And even if I wanted to leave, you need to ask me, not fucking order me."

He cocked his head to the side, those sexy strange eyes glued to mine and making me want to climb over my desk like a cat in heat and swallow his whole dick. "Kareema, I don't care if we have to bring Tori and the baby with us, you're coming with me. I don't care if I have to dig this damn building up and drag it behind a fucking eighteen-wheeler all the way to Vegas, you're coming with me. I will pack all these little kids up and take them too, but *you are coming with me*."

I opened my mouth, then dropped my eyes to the top of my desk. "You love me that much?"

I looked up to see him nod.

"Set…I—"

Before I could refuse again, he hopped up from the chair, dick swinging in his sweats. "Come on. I want you to go somewhere with me."

With my eyes stapled below his waist, I licked my lips, and said, "Okay."

*****

I thought "somewhere" meant he was taking me to my house to screw me into agreeing to leave with him which, sadly, would've probably worked. So imagine my surprise when he pulled into a parking spot in front of the Eternal Waters Care Center—a nursing home.

I was just about to ask what we were doing there when he jumped out of his rental and was opening my door in what felt like seconds. When I climbed out of the car, he grasped my hand and just started walking. The look in his eyes told me to keep my questions to myself. It wasn't a look of anger or intimidation. It was a look of...fear, of intense trepidation.

I followed him through the building as he took a path he evidently knew well, ignoring the staff's greetings and finally ending up at room three-twenty. Then he just stood and stared at the closed door.

I placed my free hand on his arm. "Set?"

His head popped up and he turned to look at me, his expression one of uncertainty. He stared at me, his eyes portraying his love for me so purely that I wondered how I'd missed it before. I gave him a smile of encouragement, because something in my soul told me he needed it. In return, he nodded and opened the door, leading me inside to reveal an older man asleep in the bed with a petite woman sitting beside him.

"Set?!" the woman squealed, but she didn't move a muscle. Neither did Set.

"Hey, Mama," Set said, giving her a tiny smile and gesturing his head toward the man. "How's he doing?"

"He's good! Well, as good as he can be. I'm

just glad he's still with us," she replied. She was a pretty woman who almost looked too young to be Set's mother.

"That's good. Uh, this is Kareema, my fiancée. Kareema, this is my mom, Charmaine Mitchell."

Fiancée? The hell?

I was ten thousand-percent sure I was looking crazy as I offered Set's mother a smile and uttered, "Um, nice to meet you, Mrs. Mitchell."

She rested a hand on her chest. "Oh, my! Fiancée? That's wonderful!"

"Yeah," Set said, his eyes glued to his sleeping—or comatose—father. "Well, I'ma head out. Just wanted to check on y'all."

Still sitting in that chair next to her husband, half a room away from her son, she chimed, "Okay! It was so good to see you!"

Then we left, my heart breaking for the man I loved as he led me back to the car.

Set

"Set?" she nearly whispered after we had climbed back into the car.

"He has dementia, doesn't know me anymore, so I'm glad he was asleep. I definitely wasn't gonna wake him up," I told her, answering a question I knew she wanted to ask.

"Oh..."

"We had to damn near force Mama to put him in there after he pulled a gun on her thinking she was a burglar one night."

I started the car and heard her say, "I'm sorry about your dad, Set. Why didn't you tell me before now?"

I looked over at her. "I don't like thinking about him like that even though he fucked me up."

She lowered her eyes. "I understand, but uh...fiancée?"

"Yep."

"Is that your way of asking me to marry you?"

"I guess you could say that."

"Okay, but why would you tell your mother I was already going to be your wife?"

"Because you are, ain't you?"

"Um, I...Set, I don't...uh..."

Reaching over to lift her chin so that she was looking at me, I asked, "You ain't gonna marry the nigga you been in love with for three damn years, Kareema?"

"Why did I tell your ass I loved you? I knew you were gonna use it against me..."

"Yeah, you fucked up, but so did I. Now you know I love you and that you got my nose wide-damn-open. I can barely sleep when we're apart. I'm ready to slit Shawn Thomas's throat over you and to adopt and re-raise your daughter. Shit, you could ask me to cut my dick off and give it to you and I'd actually think about it for two or three seconds before telling you *fuck no*. You *gotta* marry me, Kareema. And you gotta move to Vegas with me."

"Well, if we were married it wouldn't make sense for us to live in different states, but—"

"See, that's what I'm saying. So we gonna do this, move and get married. Or get married and move. The order don't matter to me, but we doing it. We doing both."

"Set Mitchell, you are the most frustrating man I have ever known! How do you think you can just *tell* me what we're going to do?! I'm a grown-ass woman!"

"Naw, I ain't the *most* frustrating man you've ever known. I know that ain't true."

"Okay, second most frustrating."

"Uh-huh."

"I told you I don't want to get married, Set."

"What the fuck does that mean? I said the same thing, but I'm about to marry your ass, ain't I?"

"Why can't you move here?"

"You know you don't wanna be here no more, Kareema. I can tell you don't."

"How?"

"I just can."

She sighed.

"I love you, Kareema."

"I love you too, but…"

"But what? And the what better not be some bullshit about you not leaving with me or not marrying me. That's not negotiable."

"Not negotiable?"

"That's what I said, ain't it?"

She blew out a breath. "Fine, I'll go to Vegas with you. I can hire someone new or promote one of the teachers to run the daycare."

"*And*?"

"*And*, where's the ring, Set?"

"What kind you want? My credit score is eight-thirteen. I got you, baby."

"You don't already have a ring?"

"Nah, I ain't know we was getting married until I found out you loved me back."

"How'd you miss that?"

"The same way you missed the fact that I will swim through lava for your ass."

That's when she started crying, and I frowned. "What is it? What's wrong, Kareema?"

Shaking her head, she whimpered, "I never thought this was possible, that I could feel this way about a man and he'd feel the same way about me. I love you so much and…yeah, I want to leave this damn city and that job I feel trapped in. I love Vegas and your place and your gym and…why'd you want me to come out there so bad after we had agreed not to visit each other's homes?"

Damn, she was all over the place, so I reached for her, hugging her across the center console. "I don't know. I guess I wanted to know how it would feel to have you in my space, my bed."

"How was it?"

"Obviously, it was good, *perfect*. Uh, Kareema?"

"Yeah?" she said into my chest.

"I really gotta get a ring for you to say yes?"

"No, but you do have to promise you'll stop fighting."

"Fighting?"

"The underground fighting you told me about? You gotta promise to stop that, because if you get hurt, I don't know what I'll do."

I squeezed my arms tighter around her. "Aw, baby. With you in my life full time, I won't need to fight."

"Okay, then I'll marry you."

"Good. Kareema?"

"Uh-huh?"

"You gotta stop crying so I can take you to your house and eat your pussy while I put my finger in your ass."

She laughed as she backed out of my arms and wiped her face. "You are so damn weird."

I grinned. "I know."

15

Kareema

Two months earlier...

Set: *I wanna see you. It's been too long.*

Me: *It's only been a couple of months.*

Set: *My balls gonna fall off if I don't get to see you.*

I laughed before responding to that text with: *You say you're trying to see me but it sounds like you're trying to see my coochie.*

Set: *Shit, I'm tryna see both of y'all! Come on. Pick a weekend and by pick a weekend, I mean this weekend.*

Me: *Set, it's Friday. Too last minute.*

Set: *Next weekend then. I need some of that.*

Me: *That?*

Set: *That PUSSY.*

Me: *Really? All caps?*

Set: *I'm just tryna put some respect on her name.*

Me: *Give me a couple of weeks at least. Where are we meeting?*

Set: *Vegas.*

I stared at the word for two or three minutes, more than a little taken aback. He wanted me to come to *his* city?

Set: *You still there?*

Me: *Yeah. What hotel in Vegas?*

Set: *The Mitchell Inn.*

Me: *You mean your place?*

Set: *Yep.*

Me: *Won't your girlfriend be upset about me being in your town and in your place?*

Set: *Is your nigga gonna be upset about you coming to my town and my place?*

Asshole.

Another two minutes passed before I typed out: *Let's do Dallas. It's closer to me.*

Set: *Vegas*

Me: *St. Louis*

Set: *Vegas*

This went on for ten more cities with me having no clue why he suddenly decided to change the rules but wanting to see him so bad that I could only say: *Fine. Vegas.*

Set: *Good. I'ma tear your ass up!*

Me: *You better.*

I spent the next month or so stalling, afraid of what being with him in his home could mean, making up excuse after excuse for the delay before I finally bought a plane ticket and flew to Vegas, to him.

Kareema
Now...

Gripping the railing on Set's—*our*—balcony, I
wanted to keep my eyes open and on the night's
scenery, but I couldn't. Set was so deep inside of
me I could damn near hear his thoughts, his dick
massaging every inch of my pussy as his body
crowded the back of mine, one hand tightly
gripping my right breast, the other on my
shoulder. His warm breath caressed my ear as
he asked, "Whose pussy is this? Huh? Whose
pussy is this, baby?"

"Shit, shit, shit! I think you're in my damn
uterus!" I replied, my pussy seizing and
squirting all at the same time.

"Yeah, make it rain for me, baby. Come for
me, Kareema."

"Oooooo, shit!"

"This motherfucker so damn tight! Got damn
boa constrictor pussy!"

And that's when he lost it, started plowing
into me like there was no tomorrow, making my
knees buckle and a cry of pure insanity fly from
my mouth.

Wrapping his arms around my waist, he
turned me around, and the next thing I knew, I
was on my back on one of the loungers and Set's
mouth was on me, slurping and sucking on my
clit and making tears spring to my eyes from the

intensity of pleasure mixed with love. He slipped a finger inside of me and my legs turned to jelly. My heart was beating out of my chest, and all kinds of nasty thoughts were swirling around in my brain.

And that's when *I* lost it, squirmed from under him, surprising him enough to give me room to take him into my mouth, swirl my tongue around his dick, and slide it so deep inside my mouth that I gagged, coughed, and grinned.

"Ooooh, fuck!" Set groaned.

We'd barely made it through his door before he stripped both of us and led me out to this balcony. It was hot, but I was naked, and the mere idea of us fucking outside gave my pussy the consistency of slush.

I sucked and slurped and gagged and sucked some more, until Set pulled me up, spun me around, and had me gripping the railing again. He drove into me, making me moan and suck in a breath at the same time, soon resuming his rhythm, his flesh smacking against mine, our breathing loud, our moans tortured, the slippery wetness of my pussy echoing around us, the scent of our sex permeating the hot night air.

A building orgasm crested inside of me, causing static to drown out the sounds of our sex. And when my hearing reverted to normalcy, my man whined and roared my name about twenty times as his throbbing dick emptied inside of me.

Set

I fell onto the lounger on my back and was about to tell her to lie down on me, but she beat me to it, stretching her body over mine, those titties smashed between us.

After I caught my breath, I said, "You ain't never tell me whose pussy it is."

"You know it's yours. I got the rings to prove it now." She held up her left hand and grinned. "I can't believe you actually drove from the airport to a jewelry store, then to a chapel."

I shrugged. "We too old to be waiting."

"All this screwing we do, and you think we're old?"

"Shit, that's that old nigga experience. You think I could fuck like this back in the day? I had no idea what I was doing."

"If that's what you mean, then you're old as hell. Shit, you're two seconds from the nursing home."

I chuckled. "Kareema?"

"Yeah?"

"I love you."

She kissed my chest and then my lips. "I love you, too. Hey, what if I told you this was somebody else's pussy and not yours when you asked?"

"Then I'd put my foot up *somebody else's* ass and shove my fist down *somebody else's* throat, and cut *somebody else's* dick off and—"

"Okay, okay, I get the point, crazy ass man!"

"Good." I reached between us and gripped her pussy. "Now who does this belong to, baby?"

She lifted her head from my chest to look me in the eye. "It belongs to Set Moses Mitchell."

"You got damn right."

A southern girl at heart, Alexandria House has an affinity for a good banana pudding, Neo Soul music, and tall black men in suits. When this fashionista is not shopping, she's writing steamy stories about real black love.

Connect with Alexandria!
Email: **msalexhouse@gmail.com**
Website: http://www.msalexhouse.com/
Newsletter: http://eepurl.com/cOUVg5
Blog: http://msalexhouse.blogspot.com/
Facebook: Alexandria House
Instagram: @msalexhouse
Twitter: @mzalexhouse

Also by Alexandria House:

Them Boys Novella Series:
Set

The McClain Brothers Series:
Let Me Love You
Let Me Hold You
Let Me Show You
Let Me Free You
Let Me Please You (A McClain Family Novella)

The Strickland Sisters Series:
Stay with Me
Believe in Me
Be with Me

The Love After Series:
Higher Love
Made to Love
Real Love

Short Stories:
Should've Been
Merry Christmas, Baby
Baby, Be Mine

Always My Baby

Text alexhouse to 555888 to be notified of new releases!